Good Idea, Amelia Jane!

Enid Blyton™

Good Idea, Amelia Jane!

 EGMONT

EGMONT

We bring stories to life

First published in Great Britain 2001 by Egmont Books Limited
239 Kensington High Street, London W8 6SA

Individual stories first published in Enid Blyton's Magazine:
ENID BLYTON® Amelia Jane's Spots text copyright © 1955 Chorion Rights Limited
ENID BLYTON® Good Idea, Amelia Jane! text copyright © 1956 Chorion Rights Limited
ENID BLYTON® Come Now, Amelia Jane! text copyright © 1956 Chorion Rights Limited
ENID BLYTON® Amelia Jane and the Sailor Doll text copyright © 1953 Chorion Rights Limited
ENID BLYTON® Oh! Amelia Jane! text copyright © 1954 Chorion Rights Limited
ENID BLYTON® Tit for Tat, Amelia Jane! text copyright © 1954 Chorion Rights Limited
ENID BLYTON® Bother You, Amelia Jane! text copyright © 1957 Chorion Rights Limited
ENID BLYTON® It's Raining, Amelia Jane! text copyright © 1955 Chorion Rights Limited
ENID BLYTON® Amelia Jane and the Keys text copyright © 1956 Chorion Rights Limited
ENID BLYTON® Amelia Jane and the Records text copyright © 1957 Chorion Rights Limited
All rights reserved

49470/2
10 9 8 7 6 5 4 3 2

A CIP catalogue record for this title is available from the British Library

Typeset by Dorchester Typesetting Group Ltd, Dorset
Printed and bound in Great Britain by the CPI Group (UK) Ltd, Croydon, CR0 4YY

Contents

Amelia Jane's Spots

'I'm very tired of Amelia Jane,' said the teddy bear. 'Very, very tired.'

'So am I,' said the clockwork mouse. 'She keeps running after me telling me not to do this and not to do that, and . . .'

'Yes, and she's always chasing *me* round, too,' said the clown. 'First she

wanted to polish up my clockwork
key, then she wanted to sew a black
bobble on my hat, then she wanted to
see if my shoes needed mending.'

'Always interfering,' said Monkey,
gloomily. 'Never still for a minute.
She kept running round after me with
a needle and cotton all day yesterday,

saying one of my
ears was coming
loose. She would
NOT leave me alone!'
'Here she comes –
hide!' said the
clockwork mouse, and
they ran off into
corners as Amelia Jane

came up. She frowned.
'Come back,' she
said, but they wouldn't.
So she went after them
all and scolded first one
and then another.

'Your whiskers need
brushing,' she told the
clockwork mouse. 'Here, let
me brush them.'

'Leave me alone!' said
the clockwork mouse. 'I
like my whiskers as they are.'

'We'll have to do *some*thing about
Amelia Jane,' said the clown,
gloomily. 'Can't *any*body make her
sit down and stay still? Let's go and

3

ask the teddy bear if he knows anything we can do.'

So they went over to the teddy bear. He had a piece of paper in front of him, and was drawing on it with coloured chalks.

'Draw Amelia Jane,' said the clockwork mouse with a giggle. So Teddy drew the big naughty doll, and he drew her really very well. When he had finished, Tom the soldier took a red chalk and put spots all over the face in the picture.

'There – she's always grumbling about me!' he said. 'Now I've given her a funny face – all spots!'

'She looks as if she's got measles,'

said Monkey, with a laugh. 'Red spots and all!'

'Oooooh!' said the little clockwork mouse, suddenly. 'Oooooh! I've got such a good idea!'

'What?' asked Tom. 'You don't usually get any ideas at all.'

'Listen!' said the mouse, excitedly. 'Why don't we wait till Amelia Jane is asleep, and then let Teddy draw red spots on her face and legs and arms? She'll think she's got measles, and she won't come near us then, in case *we* get it, too!'

'Sh! Don't talk so loudly or she'll hear you,' said Teddy. 'Really – that's quite a good idea, Mouse.'

Everyone laughed, and then Teddy set them all to keep a watch on Amelia Jane till they saw her fall asleep. Then very quietly he took the red chalk and drew little red dots and spots very gently on her face, arms and hands.

The clockwork mouse laughed so much that Monkey shut him in the brick-box till the red spots were finished. Dear me – Amelia Jane really did look most peculiar!

The toys longed for her to wake up, and at last she did. The first thing she saw was the red spots on her arms. She stared in alarm. Then she saw her red-spotted legs and gave a yell.

'I've got spots! I must have caught measles! Keep away from me, toys. Oh dear – have I got red spots on my face, too?'

'Yes. Heaps,' said the clown, with a grin. 'You look most peculiar, Amelia. Now, you must rest a lot, and not run about and tire yourself. We'll fetch you anything you want.'

'Oh dear me – how could I have caught the measles?' sighed Amelia Jane. 'Do fetch me the little mirror out of the dolls' house, Clockwork Mouse. I want to see my face.'

The mouse fetched the mirror, and

Amelia Jane looked sorrowfully at her red-spotted face. 'Well, well,' she said, 'I must be very careful not to tire myself – though I don't really feel *ill*.'

'Stay in bed,' said Teddy. 'Get into the cot and lie still, Amelia. People always go to bed with measles.'

Amelia Jane climbed into the cot and covered herself up. 'I *really* don't feel ill,' she kept saying.

'Perhaps you've only got *one* measle, not a lot of measles,' said the clockwork mouse, with one of his giggles.

'Any nonsense from you and I'll get up and chase you, measles or *not*,' said Amelia Jane at once.

Well, the toys had a really lovely time after that. Amelia Jane stayed in the cot, and sent the toys hurrying and scurrying about to fetch her this and that, but she didn't go chasing after them herself as she had done before.

Nobody minded fetching her things, if only she would stay quiet in her cot and not interfere with anything they were doing. They enjoyed the peace and quiet very much indeed.

But Amelia Jane soon began to grumble. 'I'm tired of this. I'm going to get up and wash myself today. I feel dirty. Teddy, fill the wash-basin with warm water for me.'

He filled it for her, turning on first the cold water tap, then the hot water. But Monkey went to him in alarm.

'She'll wash off the spots!' he whispered. 'Then she won't have the measles!'

But it was too late to stop Amelia from washing herself. Soon she was soaping her face, arms and legs, and then she took a towel to dry herself.

She bent down and rubbed her legs and gave a squeal.

'Oh – the spots are gone! And look, they're gone from my arms, too – and I expect they're gone from my face. I'm better again! Hurrah!'

And then she saw the red chalk marks on the clean towel, made by the red spots when she had wiped them off. She stared and stared. Then she looked round at the grinning toys.

'What's *this*?' she said, pointing to the red marks.

'Measles!' said the clockwork mouse in a hurry.

'It's *red chalk*, that's what it is!' said Amelia Jane. 'Not measles at all. Who did it? Oooh, just wait till I get down from this basin and tell you what I think of you!'

But nobody waited. They rushed
to the toy-cupboard, got in and pulled
the doors till they clicked tight. And
there they all are, wondering how
long it will take Amelia Jane to open
the doors!

What a trick to play on her!
Measles indeed!

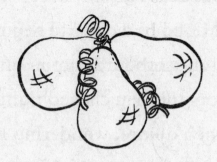

Good Idea,
Amelia Jane!

'Amelia Jane, please try not to be silly tonight,' said the big teddy bear. 'The children have left out their railway lines instead of putting them away, so we thought we'd set the trains going ourselves, just for a treat – and we don't want you to interfere.'

Amelia Jane made a face at the

bear. She was excited, because the
children had had a party that day,
and all the toys had enjoyed watching

them play games. The playroom
looked very bright because it had
balloons hung all round it, and little

paper ornaments swung here and there.

A party always made Amelia Jane feel mischievous. But now she felt cross because the bear had spoken sharply to her and told her not to interfere with them. That made her feel just *like* interfering, of course!

She waited her chance and then undid two of the toy railway lines and didn't join them up again – so the train ran right off the lines and bumped into the dolls' house with a tremendous crash! The dolls'-house dolls were very scared when they felt their house shake. 'Is it an earthquake?' they cried, and came running out in fright.

'No. It's only Amelia Jane trying to be funny,' growled the bear, putting the lines right again.

The toy monkey came out of the toy-cupboard to talk to the little station master. He spread his tail across the lines, and Amelia Jane chuckled to herself. The train was not supposed to go on the lines where Monkey's tail was, for the signal was against the train just there.

Amelia Jane had to interfere, of course! She altered the signal to make the train go a different way. It raced over the track just by Monkey – and ran over his tail!

He shot up into the air in a fright and left his tail behind him – and the train ran right off the lines when it bumped over the tail! Amelia Jane laughed and laughed.

'Amelia Jane, go and sit in the toy-cupboard and stay there!' said the bear. 'Just look at poor old

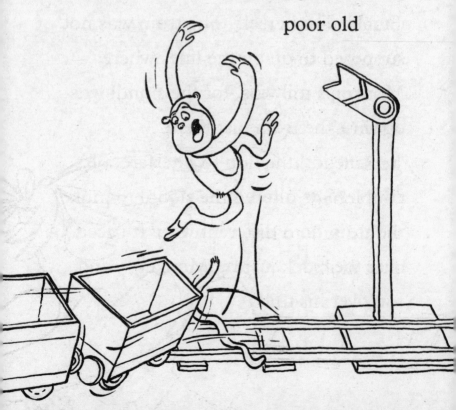

Monkey without his tail! And the train is lying on its side, all in a heap. What a pity you always have bad ideas, and never good ones. Go away, please.'

The bear was very angry, and all the other toys looked so cross that Amelia thought perhaps she had better go into the toy-cupboard. So away she went and sat down by herself.

Nobody would talk to her that night.

Nobody asked her to come and join in the games they played with the toy soldiers out of the fort. Nobody offered her a sweet when the sweet-shop man opened a little bottle of chocolate drops. She began to feel rather miserable.

Perhaps I *do* have too many bad ideas, and not enough good ones! she thought. I'll try and think of a good one for a change.

But she couldn't! So there she sat at the back of the toy-cupboard, all by herself, watching the other toys eating chocolate drops and laughing and talking.

Then suddenly someone called out

in surprise. 'It's raining! Raining in the playroom!'

Amelia Jane thought that was too silly for words! 'Rain comes from clouds in the sky, it doesn't fall *indoors*!' she called.

'Well, it does tonight!' said Tom the soldier, puzzled. 'There – I felt a drip on my nose – and look, a rain-drop just splashed on the floor near me!'

Amelia Jane came out of the toy-cupboard in surprise. 'But it *can't* rain indoors,' she began – and just at that very moment a large drop of water fell on her head! She *was* surprised! She looked up into the air – and

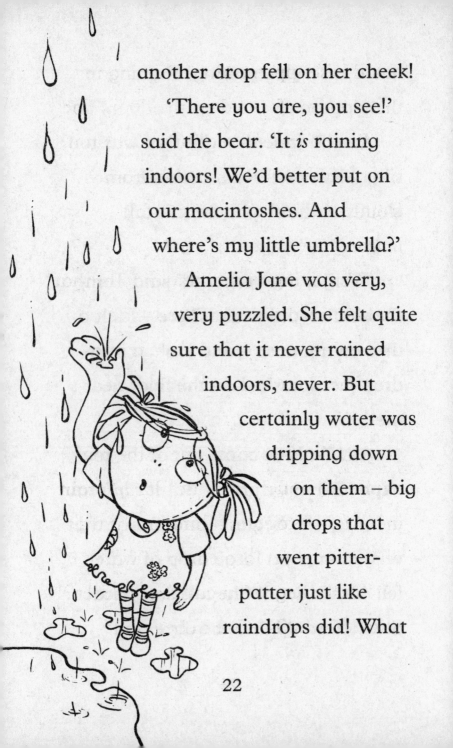

another drop fell on her cheek! 'There you are, you see!' said the bear. 'It *is* raining indoors! We'd better put on our macintoshes. And where's my little umbrella?' Amelia Jane was very, very puzzled. She felt quite sure that it never rained indoors, never. But certainly water was dripping down on them – big drops that went pitter- patter just like raindrops did! What could be happening?

A puddle formed on the floor. The clockwork mouse went to paddle in it, but soon it was so wide that he was frightened and ran into the toy-cupboard.

'It's getting bigger and bigger, that puddle,' said the bear. 'Soon the whole floor will be like a pond and then the water will run out of the door. Shall we be drowned?'

'No,' said Amelia Jane. 'It won't get deep enough for that. But it might get into the toy-cupboard, and we'd all get very wet and catch cold.'

'Shall we go and call the children?' asked Tom. 'They're in bed and asleep – but one of us could go and wake them.'

'The water's run under the door now,' said Amelia Jane. 'There will be quite a river in the passage outside. I really don't think any of us had better paddle out to the children's room. It would be dangerous.'

'Well, what *are* we to do then?' said the bear. 'We can't just stay here and do nothing. The water's getting deeper – and just listen to the splash-splash-splash!'

Certainly the falling drops did make loud splashes. The poor little clockwork mouse was most alarmed. He climbed into the dolls' cot to be out of the way of the water, and all the little dolls'-house dolls went up the stairs of their house to the small bedrooms above. They looked out of the top windows in fright.

Now – if only I could think of a *good* idea this very minute, the toys would certainly think I was clever! thought Amelia Jane, and she looked all round the playroom, trying to find a good idea. She suddenly saw the balloons swinging gently to and fro as they always did when they were blown up and hung on strings.

'Oh! *I* know!' she said. 'I've thought of a fine way to bring the children here. Let's burst the balloons!

You know what a loud BANG they make when they go pop! It would wake the children and they'd come rushing in to see who was popping their balloons!'

'Well – yes – perhaps that *is* a good idea,' said the bear. 'But it does seem an awful waste of balloons! Still – it would be better to pop a few balloons than to have the whole playroom flooded.'

'But how *can* we burst the balloons?' asked the sailor doll. 'They're so high up.'

'Now let me think,' said Amelia Jane. 'Tom, go to the work-box where needles and cottons and things are

kept and bring me the biggest
darning needle you can see. And
Bear, get me one of the big drum-
sticks from the drum over there in the
corner.'

Well, Tom brought her a big
darning-needle and the bear fetched
her the drum-stick. Then all the toys
watched solemnly while Amelia Jane
went on with her Good Idea.

She took the big needle and tied it
to the tip of the drum-stick with one of
her hair ribbons. Then she told the
toys to push one of the playroom
chairs under the first two or three
balloons. She stood on the chair on
tiptoe and reached up with the drum-

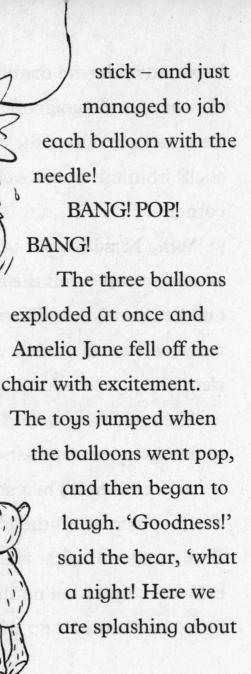

stick – and just managed to jab each balloon with the needle!

BANG! POP! BANG!

The three balloons exploded at once and Amelia Jane fell off the chair with excitement. The toys jumped when the balloons went pop, and then began to laugh. 'Goodness!' said the bear, 'what a night! Here we are splashing about

28

in water, with rain coming down from the ceiling, and balloons going bang, pop, bang overhead!'

'Push the chair along a bit,' commanded Amelia Jane, quite enjoying herself. 'Goodness, I got wet when I fell off into the water just now. Oh, be *careful*, Bear – you pushed the chair so hard that I almost fell off again!'

BANG! POP! BANG! That was three more balloons bursting when Amelia pricked them with the needle. The popping and banging went on until every one of the balloons had exploded, and were nothing but limp little bits of coloured rubber, hanging on the long string that went round the playroom walls.

'Listen! I can hear someone coming!' cried the bear, suddenly. 'Get back into the toy-cupboard, everyone – quickly! The children will be in here in half a minute.'

And then in came the two children, rubbing their sleepy eyes, and looking in astonishment at the playroom floor running with water.

'I say – what's happened? Look at all this water!' they cried. 'Mother! Dad! Quick, the house is being flooded!'

Soon the playroom was full of astonished people. The children's mother looked up at the ceiling from which big glistening drops fell continually.

'The water's coming from the bathroom!' she cried. 'Someone has left the bath-tap running. Oh dear – what a dreadful thing! The ceiling will be down in a minute! Children, go up and turn off the tap!'

The water was soon turned off in the bathroom and the children came downstairs again. 'Yes – the bath was full, and the taps were still on,' they said. 'Whoever was so very careless? It wasn't *us*, Mother!'

'How did you *know* about the water in the playroom?' asked their father. 'Did the splashing noise wake you?'

'No,' said the children. 'We didn't hear *that*! We woke up when we heard a lot of pops and bangs – like little guns going off!'

'Dear me – see – all the balloons have burst!' said their mother. '*That* must have been what you heard. But who popped them? And do look – here's a drum-stick with a darning-needle tied to it! Now *who* has been using that?'

The toys knew, of course, and they whispered together in the cupboard.

'It was Amelia Jane! Amelia, you thought of a good idea at last! Why

don't you *always* think of good ideas
instead of silly ones? You know,
you've saved us all from being
drowned tonight!'

'Well – as a matter of fact, I *have*
just thought of another good idea,'
said Amelia Jane, at once.

'What is it?' asked the bear. 'Do
tell us, Amelia, and then you can go
and do it.'

'Right!' said Amelia Jane. 'Well, *I*
think it would be a very good idea if I
creep out of the cupboard and go to
the toy sweet-shop and finish up ALL
the chocolate drops that are left!'

And dear me, the toys didn't
like to say that it wasn't *at all* a good

idea, so there goes Amelia Jane to the little sweet-shop, and that will be the last of those delicious little chocolate drops!

Come Now, Amelia Jane!

You remember Amelia Jane, don't you
– the big naughty doll who lives with
the toys in the playroom? Well, one
day she got into such trouble that she
very nearly ran away and never came
back!

She quarrelled with the tiny bear
called Grunt who lived with the dolls

in the dolls' house. He was as small as they were, and such a kind, comical little fellow that the tiny dolls in the dolls' house were delighted to have him there.

He slept in the kitchen rocking-chair, and helped to keep the dolls' house clean. 'He never minds *what* he does!' said Mandy, one of the tiny dolls. 'Why, he even tried to sweep the chimney the other day. It was a pity he poked the chimney right off the roof with his brush – but still, he soon climbed up and put it on again!'

Amelia Jane and Grunt the little bear had a very silly quarrel.

A blue button came off Amelia's

dress and rolled across the floor. She
didn't know that it had come off, and
when someone told her that she had
lost a button, she went hunting all
over the place for it.

'Wherever can it be?' she said,
looking under the hearth-rug,
and in the
fender, and
in every

corner of the room. 'It's such a dear
little button, and matches the rest of
the ones on my dress. I really must

find it. Hasn't *anyone* seen it?'

Nobody brought her the button, and Amelia Jane gave up the search. But someone *had* seen it. It was Grunt, the little dolls'-house bear. He had found it lying by the small wooden house when he had opened the front door to sweep the steps one morning. He didn't know that it was a button; it seemed very big indeed to him. It had two holes in it, where the cotton thread had gone through when it was sewn on to Amelia Jane's dress. Grunt couldn't think why the lovely blue thing had holes in it like that.

'I shall wear it round my neck,' he said. So he asked Mandy, the tiny

doll, if she had a little bit of blue silk
to thread it on.

'Then I can wear the lovely blue
thing round my neck like a locket,' he
said. 'I haven't any clothes, so it will
be nice to wear this blue thing.'

Mandy threaded a little length of
blue silk through the holes, and tied it
round Grunt's neck. 'Does it look
nice?' he said. 'It's under my furry
chin, so I can't see it, Mandy.'

'You look grand,' said Mandy,
who was very fond of the little bear.
'Perhaps it's a bead, Grunt, fallen out
of the bead-box. It's very pretty.'

Grunt felt quite important for a
day or two, wearing the blue button

under his chin on the thin silk thread. Everyone told him how nice he looked.

And then suddenly Amelia Jane saw the tiny bear, and her eye was caught by the blue button under his chin.

'What's that you've got?' she said, bending down to look. 'Oh, you bad wicked bear – it's my blue button – my lost blue button! You've stolen it!'

'I have not,' said the bear, angrily. 'As if I would steal

*any*thing! It's not a button. Mandy says it's a bead fallen out of the bead-box. It's mine. I'm wearing it.'

'It is not yours,' said Amelia Jane, in a temper. 'Look – it matches the rest of my buttons. I tell you you're a thief, Grunt. *Everyone* knew I'd lost that button, and you must have known, too.'

'Well, I didn't – and I won't give it back to you, because you said I'd stolen it,' said Grunt, stoutly. 'I shall wear it till you say you're very, very sorry for being so rude to me. I'm not a thief. Everyone knows that.'

'You are, you are!' cried Amelia. 'You know it's mine, and you won't give it back!'

'I will if you say you're very, very, VERY sorry,' said Grunt, holding his paw over the button in case Amelia Jane snatched it away.

'You just wait,' said Amelia Jane. 'Why *should* I say I'm sorry? I won't! And if you don't hand it back, I'll punish you.'

'Pooh!' said Grunt, and walked into the dolls' house and slammed the front door. Amelia Jane was furious. The clockwork mouse, who had been listening, gave one of his little giggles and that made Amelia Jane angrier still. She chased the mouse till his clockwork ran down.

'Oh, do sit down and be quiet, Amelia,' said Tom. 'Let's have a bit of peace, for goodness' sake. Who cares about your silly button? Let Grunt keep it – it suits him, and it's the only thing he's ever had to wear.'

Amelia Jane sulked. She sat in a corner and planned what to do to Grunt. She waited till all the toys were in the toy-cupboard and asleep, and then she went to the dolls' house. She looked in at the kitchen window. She saw little Grunt there, asleep in the rocking-chair.

Very quietly she pushed open the little window. She put in her big hand – and caught hold of the tiny bear!

He gave a frightened grunt, but nobody heard him. Amelia lifted him out through the window and ran to a corner of the room, so that she wouldn't wake any of the toys.

'Now you give me my button and say you're very sorry!' she said, in a loud whisper.

'I won't, you bad, unkind doll!' said the bear. 'And if you don't let me go I'll bite your fingers!'

'Oh, you bad little bear!' said Amelia Jane, and she snapped the thread that held the button under Grunt's chin, and put it into her pocket. 'There – I've got the button. Now say you're sorry, or I'll drop you into this waste-paper basket!'

'I *shan't* say I'm sorry!' said Grunt, and began to wriggle for all he was worth, and to grunt as loudly as he could. But he was only a very tiny bear, and made very tiny grunts, so nobody heard him at all. And what do you think Amelia Jane did? She kept her word, and dropped him right into the big waste-paper basket! He fell among all kinds of things – torn-up paper, apple-peel, an old cardboard box, some rags, a broken pencil, and a few dead flowers!

'Pooh!' he said. 'Take me out. It smells!'

But Amelia Jane pushed him right

to the bottom and piled everything on top of him. He was such a very little bear that he was quite squashed and could hardly move. He began to grunt as loudly as he could. 'Help! Grunt-grunt! Help!'

But everyone was sound asleep and didn't hear a single grunt. Amelia went off to her cot, climbed into it, and fell asleep, too. In the morning, when she heard someone coming into the room to clean it, she watched to see what happened. Would Jane the cleaner see Grunt in the waste-paper basket and take him out? No, she didn't – she just cleaned the room, then picked up her brush, duster and the waste-paper basket, and went off with them.

Good! thought the naughty doll. Now he can't tell anyone what I did! She fetched a needle and thread and sewed the blue button on her frock. There – now it looked nice again!

Mandy, the tiny doll, came out of the dolls' house, looking worried. 'Where's Grunt?' she said. 'He's gone.'

'Gone! Impossible!' said Tom the
soldier, and soon the toys were
looking everywhere for him. Amelia
Jane didn't look, of course. She just
watched them all.

'Why don't you help, Amelia
Jane?' asked the sailor doll. 'Poor little
Grunt – he's quite disappeared.'

'I don't care!' said Amelia Jane.
'He stole my blue button and
wouldn't say he was sorry.'

'Why – you've *got* your blue

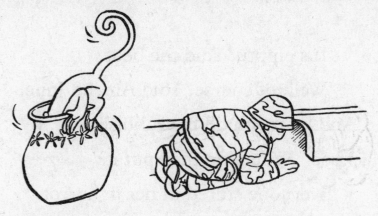

button!' cried the big teddy bear, coming up to look. 'You've sewn it on. So you must have seen Grunt and got it from him. Where is he?'

'He wouldn't say he was sorry, so I put him into the waste-paper basket,' said Amelia Jane.

'Oh, you bad doll!' cried the bear, and ran to the corner where the waste-paper basket stood. It had been emptied and brought back again. The bear and Tom peeped into it.

'It's empty,' said the bear.

'Well, of course,' said Amelia Jane. 'And he's with all the rubbish now, I expect. Where do they put it?'

Everyone stared at her in horror. 'Don't you *know* where waste-paper baskets are emptied?' said Tom at last.

'No,' said Amelia Jane.

'Well – they are emptied into the dustbin,' said Tom solemnly. 'And that's where broken toys are put – and they never, never come back again!'

'Oh! I didn't know that!' cried the big doll. 'I didn't, I didn't. Oh, I didn't mean him to go to the dustbin! I thought he'd just be tipped out somewhere and be brought back. Oh, I wouldn't have sent him to the dustbin, I really wouldn't!'

'You are horrid and unkind,' said the big teddy bear. 'The dustbin is a terrible place for any toy to go to. We are all afraid of that. And now you have sent our dear, kind little Grunt there. Amelia Jane, we will none of us ever speak to you again. We will never, never be friends with you.'

'Never, never, never!' cried all the toys loudly, and turned their backs on the big, scared doll. She really was very upset. She hadn't known that waste-paper baskets were emptied into dustbins. She couldn't *bear* to think of poor little Grunt out there in the yard, buried in a mass of rubbish, never, never to come back and play in the dolls' house again.

Nobody spoke to Amelia Jane all that day, and Mandy and the dolls'-house dolls sat and wept in the kitchen of the little dolls' house. Amelia cried, too. She really was ashamed of what she had done, and she couldn't *think* what to do. She almost made up her mind to run away and never come back!

That night, when the house was dark and quiet and the moon shone through the window, Amelia Jane suddenly stood up.

She went to the window and climbed on to the sill. Outside grew a big pear tree. Amelia slid through the open window and on to a branch. Then she began to climb down the tree.

'I hope I don't fall!' she said. 'It's the first time I ever climbed down a tree. Oh dear – I shall never come to the bottom!'

She came to it at last and there she was, on the garden path. Now – where was the yard and the dustbin? She set off in the moonlight, and soon came to the little back yard – and there, in the corner, was the big, smelly dustbin. A large black cat was there, too. He hissed at Amelia Jane.

'What do you want? Go away!'

'Oh please, big cat, can you take the lid off the dustbin for me?' begged Amelia Jane. 'There's something I want out of it.'

'I'm just going to take the lid off it for myself,' said the cat. 'I can smell bits of kippers in there – but don't you dare to eat them, or I'll scratch you.'

'I only want a tiny toy bear,' said Amelia Jane. 'Scrape up the rubbish a bit, cat, and see if you can find him for me.'

CRASH! The cat sent the big lid flying and then jumped into the dustbin. He began to scrape vigorously at the rubbish inside, and out on to the ground it fell – and Amelia Jane found herself covered with all kinds of smelly bits and pieces!

And then suddenly something landed beside her with a funny little grunt. It was the tiny bear.

'Oh! *Grunt!* Dear Grunt!' cried Amelia Jane in delight. 'I came to rescue you. Quick, come with me to the old pear-tree, and I'll help you to climb up. I'm very, very sorry I put you into the waste-paper basket – I really didn't know it was emptied into the dustbin! Oh dear – how you do smell!'

She helped the tiny bear up the tree and into the playroom. She took him to the dolls' house and opened the door for him. 'Go and have a bath,' she whispered. 'You'll be all right in the morning. And I'll leave you a little present on the doorstep, so look for it when you wake up.'

The little bear went to have a bath in the tiny bathroom. He rubbed himself dry, glad to be out of that dreadful dustbin. Then he sat in his little rocking-chair in the kitchen and fell fast asleep.

In the morning he remembered what Amelia had said, and went to look on the doorstep – and what do you think was there?

A necklace made from all the blue buttons off the big doll's dress! Yes, Amelia had cut them off and threaded them together to make a necklace for the bear. He put it on at once and felt very, very grand.

Then he ran to tell the toys the

story of how Amelia Jane had rescued him from the dustbin in the middle of the night, and had given him a lovely necklace made of all the buttons from her dress!

Dear me, Amelia Jane was quite a heroine after that, and she and Grunt are good friends now.

But you never know with Amelia – a heroine one night, and into mischief the next! We'll just wait and see how you behave now, Amelia Jane!

Amelia Jane and the Sailor Doll

Once a new sailor doll came to the playroom where Amelia Jane and the rest of the toys lived. He was such a chatterbox.

'You know, sailors have adventures, plenty of them,' he said. 'And you should just hear mine . . .'

'We don't want to,' said Amelia

Jane. 'You've told us about twenty times already.'

'You're the rudest doll I've ever met,' said the sailor doll, huffily. 'Well, as I was saying – one day when I was out at sea in my ship – I was the captain, of course – an enormous storm blew up, and the ship rocked to and fro, to and fro, just like a . . .'

'Rocking-horse,' said Amelia with a giggle.

'Please be quiet,' said the sailor. 'Well, I somehow steered the ship to land and everyone was saved. Another time I went out in a lifeboat to rescue two people who couldn't swim. I got a medal for that. Look.'

'It's not a medal,' said Amelia Jane. 'It's a button you picked up at the back of the toy-cupboard. It's been there for ages.'

'I don't believe you've ever *been* in a ship or a boat,' said the clockwork mouse. 'You just talk and talk.'

Well, the sailor doll wasn't going to stand any rudeness from the mouse and he chased him all round the room. Then he made a face at Amelia Jane and turned his back on her. He began talking all over again.

'*How* can we stop Sailor from going on and on about adventures I'm sure he never had?' said the teddy bear. 'He's like a record that won't stop.'

Well, Sailor went on like that till a day came when the children took the toys out into the garden for a picnic. They took little chairs and tables, too, for the toys to sit on, and gave them tiny cups of lemonade, and plates full of biscuit crumbs. The toys really enjoyed themselves.

After the picnic the children went indoors and left the toys by themselves. They were beside the little round pond where water-lilies floated

on the water. Amelia Jane wanted to take off her shoes and paddle in the water. She called to the sailor doll.

'Come on, Sailor! You love the water, don't you? Let's paddle up to our knees – and you could take off your suit and have a swim if you wanted to.'

'I don't want to,' said the sailor.

'You could sit on a water-lily leaf and have a very nice time,' said Teddy.

'Don't be silly,' said Sailor.

'Well, just come and wet your toes,' said Tom the soldier. 'Come on – you're always talking about what a wonderful life it is on the water – here's plenty for you!'

'I'm sleepy,' said the sailor doll. 'Leave me alone. I wish there was somewhere soft and cosy to curl up on – I'd have a nap in the sun.'

Amelia Jane stared at him and a wicked look came into her eyes. 'I know what you can do!' she said. 'Look!'

She took hold of the toy table and

turned it upside down. She took some
small cushions off the toy chairs and
tucked them into the upside-down
table. It looked a bit odd with its four
legs sticking up into the air.

'A nice cosy bed for you!' said
Amelia to Sailor. 'Get in and have a
nap. You *do* look tired.'

Sailor was surprised to have so
much kindness from Amelia Jane. He
got into the table-bed and lay down.

He yawned loudly.

'Nobody is to disturb
me,' he said.

'No, your Majesty,' said the
clockwork mouse with a giggle. Sailor
frowned and closed his eyes.

'Don't disturb him,' whispered
Amelia Jane to the others. 'Let him go
fast asleep.' They were all puzzled.
Why was Amelia being so nice to the
sailor doll? Nobody liked him much.
'I'll tell you in a minute,' she
whispered.

Soon the sailor doll began to
snore. He often snored, and usually
Amelia Jane pinched him to stop him.
But she didn't this time. She tiptoed
to the table-bed and smiled all over
her face. She beckoned to Teddy,
Tom and the clockwork clown.

'We'll carry the upside-down table to the pond,' she whispered. 'And we'll set it floating on the water like a little boat. Whatever will he say when he wakes up?'

The clockwork mouse giggled so loudly that the bear gave him a sharp push. 'Be quiet! You'll wake Sailor!'

Very gently the four toys each took one leg of the table and carried it to the pond. They set it down on the water and Amelia gave it a push. It floated off beautifully to the middle of the pond, bumping into a yellow water-lily as it went. The goldfish were very surprised. They popped their red noses out of the water and had a good look.

'There he goes,' said Amelia Jane, with a chuckle. 'He's got a boat at last! Hallo, Captain! Hey, Captain, wake up, you're on a voyage to far lands!'

The sailor doll woke up with a jump. He frowned. Hadn't he told the toys he wasn't to be disturbed? He turned over crossly on his cushions, and put one hand out over the edge of the floating table.

He got a sudden shock. Goodness! He had put his hand into something cold and wet! He sat up in a hurry.

He gazed round in fright. He was

bobbing on the pond! Goodness
gracious, what had happened! Why,
the land seemed a long, long way
away! He saw the toys standing on
the edge of the pond, laughing.

'How did I get here?' he shouted.
'Save me, quick!'

'You're the captain of your boat!'
shouted Amelia. 'You're sailing far
away. You're having an adventure!
Ooooh – mind a storm doesn't blow up!'

'I don't like it!' wailed Sailor,
clinging to one of the table-legs. 'I
feel sick.'

'He's sea-sick,' said the clockwork
mouse.

'No, pond-sick,' said Teddy, with a

grin. 'Our brave and wonderful Sailor, who has been through so many marvellous adventures, feels sea-sick on the pond. Hallo – here comes the rain!'

Plop, plop, plop! Great rain-drops fell on Sailor. The wind blew a little and ripples came on the pond. The table-boat bobbed up and down and sailed all by itself into the very middle of the water-lilies.

'Help! Help!' yelled Sailor. 'I shall drown! I shall fall in and drown!'

'Swim then!' shouted Tom, enjoying himself. 'Swim like you say you do when you go and rescue people.'

'I can't swim!' wailed Sailor. 'I can't, I can't! Save me!'

'The table's bobbing about on those little waves – I think it will turn over,' said the clockwork clown. 'Hey, Sailor! Your boat may sink! Get out and sit on one of those water-lily leaves – they are nice and flat!'

Sailor really was afraid that his table-boat would sink. He jumped on to a big, flat water-lily leaf. He sat down on it – and immediately it started to sink beneath him, and there he was, sitting in the water, yelling at the top of his voice.

'Goodness. He'll drown! He really and truly *can't* swim, for all the tales

he's told us!' said the bear, suddenly.
'Look, he's slipping off that leaf – he's
right in the water!'

And will you believe it, the fat old
teddy bear suddenly plunged into the
pond and began to swim as fast as he
could towards poor old Sailor! Wasn't
it brave of him?

Sailor clutched hold of him and
Teddy swam back, puffing and
panting. All the toys
crowded round. They
patted Teddy on his
dripping wet back, and
told him he was very,
very brave.

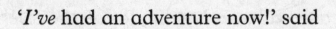

'*I've* had an adventure now!' said

Teddy, trying to squeeze water out of his furry little ears. 'I swam out and saved somebody.'

'Yes. But *your* adventure is a true one and Sailor's never are,' said Amelia Jane. 'Are they, Sailor?'

Sailor was standing all alone, his clothes making a puddle of wetness round his feet. He looked very much ashamed of himself. 'Thank you, Teddy,' he said in a small voice. 'You

were very brave – braver than I've ever been.'

'That's the way to talk!' said Tom, pleased. 'Come on – the sun's out again, so you and Teddy can sit in this sunny corner and get dry. Whatever will the children say when they find you dripping wet?'

Well, both Teddy and Sailor were dry when the children came back – but the little table still floated upside down on the pond! How surprised they were to see it there.

'Cushions in it, too!' they said. 'What *have* the toys been up to?'

The toys didn't say a word, of course, but Amelia Jane looked even naughtier than usual.

And now when Sailor forgets himself and begins one of his tales, Teddy interrupts at once, in a very loud voice, and begins his own tale.

'Once I swam out to rescue a silly sailor doll who couldn't even *swim*. It was a wonderful adventure for me. I'll tell you all about it.'

And then, of course, Sailor stops boasting at once and creeps away. A sailor doll who can't swim! He will never, never be allowed to forget that.

What naughty things you do, Amelia Jane! However do you think of them?

Oh! Amelia Jane!

Once all the toys in the nursery were very pleased because Amelia Jane had gone away for a little while. The children who owned the toys had taken her when they went to stay with their cousins.

'It's really *peaceful* without Amelia Jane!' said Tom the soldier. 'Nobody going round teasing us. . .'

'Nobody boasting, nobody pulling

tails,' said the teddy bear.

'She always thinks she's so clever, but she isn't really,' said the clockwork clown.

Just as he was speaking a small mouse scurried out of the hole in the wall, squeaking loudly.

'Eee, eee, eee! Help me, help me!'

'Whatever's the matter?' said the toys, in alarm.

'I went too near the bonfire out in the garden, and I've burnt my whiskers off!' wept the mouse. 'Can you get me some more? I feel awful.'

The toys looked at him. The clockwork mouse gave a tiny giggle.

'You look funny,' he said. 'Your

face looks undressed without whiskers,
Mouse.'

'Don't laugh at me,' begged the
mouse. 'My family keep pointing their
paws at me and giggling, and I can't
bear it. Please do get me some
whiskers.'

'We haven't any,' said the bear.
'We don't keep a store of them in the
cupboard, silly!'

'Well, I can't go back to my
family,' said the mouse, and dropped
some tiny tears on to the carpet.

'Could you lend me something to tie up my face, as if I had the toothache – then nobody would know I had lost my whiskers, and they would be sorry for me.'

'All right,' said Tom, turning away to hide a smile. 'If you think you'll look nicer all tied up for toothache, we'll find something for you. Let me see – what could you have?'

'There's a blue hanky belonging to Amelia Jane in that box over there,' said the golden-haired doll. 'As she's away she won't be wanting it. We could tie up the mouse's face with that.'

So they got the blue hanky and tied up the mouse's little face, so that

only his little twitchy
nose and bright eyes
could be seen.
He really
looked rather
sweet. He
ran down
the hole to

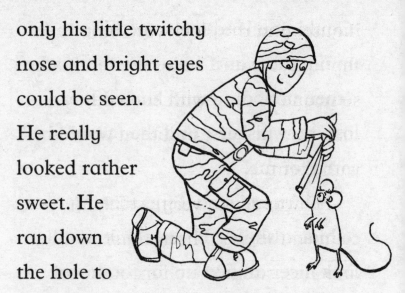

his family – but in two minutes' time
he was back again.

'They laughed at me more than
ever!' he wept. 'They rolled on the
floor with laughing. I shan't live with
them, the unkind things. If I do odd
jobs for you, may I live up here with
you – *please*?'

Well, everyone liked the little

mouse, and the clockwork mouse thought it would be lovely to have someone to play with each day, so they said yes, the mouse could live with them.

He was really very useful. He cleaned the dolls' house thoroughly, and even swept the chimney. He combed out the golden-haired doll's curls for her each day. He polished the little wooden

engine till it shone. The toys were very pleased to have him. They soon got used to seeing him with his face tied up in Amelia's blue hanky. He was sometimes very sad about his lost whiskers, and then he would go into the empty brick-box and cry in a corner. The teddy bear had to keep fetching him out to comfort him.

And then one day the children came back from their long stay away and brought Amelia Jane with them. They sat her down in the nursery and left her while they went to play in the garden.

'Hallo!' said Amelia Jane, looking round. 'How small this place seems – and what a miserable lot of toys you look, after the ones I've been used to! I can tell you, I've . . .'

'We don't want to hear, if you've only come back to boast and to find fault with us,' said the clockwork clown, quite hurt. 'We got on very well without you – in fact, we didn't miss you at all.'

Amelia Jane was the one to feel hurt then! 'What!' she said, 'you didn't miss me – and I'm the cleverest toy in the nursery! I was always the one to think up tricks and jokes!'

'Well, we did very well without them,' said the bear. 'Very well indeed. You're not *really* clever! You only think you are.'

'This is a very horrid welcome home,' said Amelia Jane. 'I thought you'd be so pleased to see me. Hallo – who's this peculiar little fellow with his face all tied up?'

'It's the mouse who lives down the hole – don't you remember him?' said Tom. 'He burnt his whiskers off, and he was so ashamed to be seen without them that we tied up his face in a hanky.'

'*My* hanky, too, I see,' said Amelia Jane. 'Give it back at once.'

'No! No!' said the mouse, backing away. 'I can't bear to be seen without whiskers.'

'Give it back,' said Amelia. 'How long have you worn it?'

'About three weeks,' said the mouse, beginning to cry again.

'Now don't make my hanky wet,' said Amelia Jane. 'I must say this is a miserable home-coming – nobody pleased to see me, and my hanky – my *best* hanky – being worn by a mouse.'

'Don't be unkind to him,' said the clockwork mouse. 'He's been very very useful to us, and he's a good little mouse.'

'I'm *not* going to be unkind to him!' said Amelia Jane. 'Quite the opposite. I'm going to say a few magic words to bring all his whiskers back – and when he takes off my hanky, hey presto, he'll have just as good a set of whiskers as ever he had!'

'Fibber!' said the bear. 'You always say you know magic, but you don't.'

'Right. Well, just see,' said Amelia Jane, with a sudden giggle. She waved her hands in the air, tapped the mouse on the nose, and said 'Wiffly-woffly, willabee, woo, may your whiskers come back to YOU!'

The mouse stared at her in

excitement. 'Oh – take off the hanky! Perhaps they've come back!'

The bear stepped forward and untied the blue hanky, quite certain that this was one of Amelia Jane's jokes. He whipped the hanky off the mouse's face.

And will you believe it, he had the finest whiskers you ever saw! How everyone stared!'

'There you are,' said Amelia Jane. 'I told you so!'

The mouse rushed at her and tried to hug her ankle, the only part of her he could reach. 'Oh, thank you, thank you! You're the kindest, cleverest toy I've ever seen in my life. I *am* so glad you've come back. Oh, my whiskers, just *look* at my whiskers!'

The toys stared as if they couldn't believe their eyes. Yes – the mouse certainly had some very fine whiskers indeed – what a wonderful thing!

'You're a marvel, Amelia Jane,' said the bear. 'How did you do it?'

'How clever you are!' said Tom the soldier. 'I *am* glad you've come home again.'

'Good old Amelia Jane!' said the clockwork clown, turning head-over-heels three times running. 'Three cheers for the cleverest doll in the world!'

Amelia Jane beamed round at everyone. 'Ah, I thought you'd soon change your minds when I'd been with you for a few minutes,' she said.

She began to play with the toys – but every now and again she went into the toy-cupboard by herself and shut the door. Nobody knew why. The bear peeped through the key-hole and tiptoed back to the others.

'She's laughing to herself,' he told

them. 'Laughing and laughing and laughing! What about, do you suppose?'

Well, *you* know of course, don't you? Amelia Jane didn't make the mouse's whiskers come back – they had grown again under the blue hanky, just as whiskers always do! And every time the big naughty doll thought of how she had tricked all the toys, she had to go away and laugh.

Oh, Amelia Jane – you and your magic words! Wiffly-woffly, willabee, woo!

Tit for Tat, Amelia Jane!

In the nursery there was an old bear on wheels. He was so old that he had belonged to the children's grandmother when *she* was a little girl.

The toys didn't take much notice of him, because he was so often asleep. 'I'm too old to stay awake for long,' he said. 'And toys are so silly nowadays – and their manners are shocking. Now when I was a young bear . . .'

But nobody wanted to hear how sensible and well-mannered toys were when the bear was young. They laughed at him and left him alone in his dark little corner.

Sometimes he was lonely – but he wouldn't ask the toys to play with him or talk to him. He didn't like any of them, and he especially disliked Amelia Jane, the big naughty doll, because she liked to sit on his back and jiggle him along on his wheels.

So there he stood, asleep most of

the time, and nobody ever played with him. Then one day a little boy came into the nursery with his mother and saw the old bear.

'I want to ride him!' he said, and mounted the bear's hairy back. 'Look, Mummy – what's this ring in his back for?'

'Oh – that used to make him growl when the children pulled it,' said his mother. So the little boy pulled at the ring – but the bear had forgotten how to growl, so he didn't make any noise at all.

The little boy tugged harder still – and suddenly the ring and the chain it was fastened to came right out of the bear's back, and left a hole there!

'There now!' said the boy's mother. 'Look what you've done! Still – that old bear hasn't growled for years. Give me the ring and chain. I'll throw them away – they're rusty.'

They went out of the room and the bear was left standing there, with a hole in his back. The toys didn't know what had happened, and they didn't care, either. Nobody bothered about the cross old bear!

It was Amelia Jane who found the hole in his back. She went to sit on

him and annoy him, and suddenly
saw the little round hole there. She
slipped her fingers into it, in surprise.

'Don't,' said the bear.

'Why? Does it hurt?' asked Amelia.

'No. It tickles,' said the bear.
'Don't do it. I'll shake you off my
back if you do.'

'No, please don't,' said Amelia
Jane, getting off quickly. She had
bumped her head the last time the
bear had shaken her off, and she
hadn't liked it.

She didn't think any more about
the hole in the bear's back till the next
night. She quarrelled with the sailor
doll, and snatched his hat off his

head! She ran away with it and he
ran after her.

'Give me back my hat!' he yelled.

'Not till you've said you're sorry
you were rude to me!' shouted back
Amelia Jane.

'I wasn't, and I shan't!' cried the sailor doll in a rage and chased Amelia Jane round the nursery. She ran to the little dark corner where the old bear stood, wondering where she could hide the sailor's hat. She suddenly remembered the hole in the bear's back!

In a moment she had stuffed the hat into it and it fell down into the bear's middle. Amelia Jane ran out into the middle of the room, laughing. 'I've hidden it. You'll never find it!'

The sailor doll went into the corner and hunted. He couldn't find his hat *any*where. He woke up the sleepy old bear. 'Listen, bear!' he said, 'did you see where that naughty doll hid my hat?'

'Your hat? I didn't even know you wore one,' said the bear. 'I've no idea *where* it is!'

That made Amelia Jane giggle, though nobody knew why. The sailor doll gave up looking after a bit. He was sad not to have his hat – and very angry with Amelia Jane.

Amelia was pleased to think she had found such a grand hidey-hole. She hid all kinds of things there! She put a brooch there belonging to the golden-haired doll. She took some coins away from Tom, and emptied them into the hole, too. When they rattled down into his tummy the bear woke up in a fright. Whatever was happening?

Nobody knew of the hidey-hole. Amelia Jane kept it a secret. She wondered how much the bear could hold. It would be fun to fill him up and make him so heavy that nobody could move him! Oh, Amelia Jane, what things you do think of!

A saucepan out of the doll's house went into the hole. A piece of ribbon belonging to the pink rabbit went there, too, and three marbles from the back of the toy-cupboard. One of Tom's boots was popped inside the bear as well.

'Where's my boot gone?' said Tom, looking all round in surprise. 'Amelia Jane – have you taken it?'

'Yes,' she said. 'I took it because you scolded me this morning.'

'Well, you shouldn't pull the clockwork mouse's tail,' said Tom. 'Give me my boot.'

'I shan't. And I'll take your other boot and hide it with the first one,' said Amelia.

'What's come over you lately?' said the teddy bear, surprised. 'You're always taking things and hiding them. Where's this wonderful hidey-hole? I've looked all over the place for it!'

'That's a secret,' said Amelia Jane. 'It's very, very useful to have a hidey-hole that nobody knows about!'

Nobody would ever have found out where the hole was if Amelia hadn't quarrelled with the toy monkey. He asked her to sew one of his ears on because it had come off – and dear me, she sewed the ear on to the middle of his forehead! An ear on a forehead! What next!

The monkey was so angry that he picked up the needle and chased Amelia Jane all round the room with it.

'I'll show you what *I* can do with a needle,' he shouted, and pricked

Amelia Jane on the arm. How she squealed! She snatched at the monkey's tail and gave it such a tug that it came off in her hand. She stared at it in delight.

I'll hide it in the hidey-hole! she thought, and raced for the bear's corner. In no time she had stuffed it down the hole in his back. When the monkey came scampering over, his tail was nowhere to be seen.

'Where's my tail?'

'Find it yourself,' said Amelia. 'And don't prick me with that needle again or I'll never, never tell you where your tail is! Oooh – you do look funny with an ear growing out of your forehead!'

The monkey hunted and hunted for his tail. He hunted all night long, and he was still hunting when all the toys were fast asleep.

I *know* she put it somewhere in this corner, he thought. I know she did. I wonder if it's underneath the old bear. I'll move him and look.

But when he tried to move the bear, he couldn't! The bear was far too heavy, because he had so many things inside him, put there by naughty Amelia Jane!

Goodness – what's made the bear so heavy all of a sudden? thought the monkey, surprised. I used to be able to push him along quite easily. 'Bear, wake up.'

'Leave me alone,' said the bear, sleepily. 'It's bad enough to have Amelia Jane climbing up on my back without you bothering me too!'

'Why does she keep getting on your back?' wondered the monkey. 'I'll sit on you myself and see!'

So up he got – and the first thing he saw, of course, was the hole. He put his hand inside – but he couldn't get anything out, because everything had fallen right down inside the bear's middle.

'Don't,' said the bear. 'You tickle! Please don't!'

The monkey felt very cross. How wicked of Amelia Jane to stuff things belonging to other people down into the old bear's tummy! No wonder nobody could ever find anything she took away. He went to tell Amelia Jane what he thought of her.

But she was asleep in her cot. Beside her, on a chair, was a new dress that one of the children had made her – a lovely dress in blue silk. Amelia Jane was going to a party with the children next day, and she was going to wear it.

I'll look finer than any other doll there! she thought. The monkey stood and looked at the dress. Then he grinned all over his cheerful face. He picked up the dress from the chair and tiptoed off with it to the bear's corner.

He sat up on the bear's back and he pushed the silk dress into the hole there – he pushed it right down, as far as ever he could. It dropped down into the bear's tummy and lay there with all the other things.

Amelia Jane was dreadfully upset when she found that her dress was gone. She was sure that Monkey had taken it.

'Well, I *did*,' said Monkey. 'I hid it.'

'Where?' demanded Amelia Jane.

'In the same place that you hid my tail,' said Monkey. Amelia stared at him in horror.

'What! You put my dress inside the bear? How *dare* you? Go and get it.'

'I can't. I've stuffed it down too far – just as you stuffed my tail!' said Monkey. 'Now you can't go to the party!'

'But I must, I must!' wailed Amelia Jane.

'Go in your old dress then,' said Tom. 'It serves you right, Amelia Jane.'

So she had to go in her old dress, and she didn't like it a bit. When she had gone, Monkey did something rather clever. He went to the toy-cupboard and found an old fishing game belonging to the children. In the

box were four little fishing-rods with
hooks on the end. Monkey took one.

'What are you going to do with
that fishing-rod, Monkey?' asked the
bear.

'Watch and see,' said Monkey, and
he went to the old bear. He sat on his
back and let down the fishing-rod
string into the hole, and
then pulled it up again.
The hook had caught
Amelia Jane's new
dress! There it
was, coming up
through the hole!
The toys laughed.

'But surely

you're not going to give it back to her, are you?' said Tom. 'She really does need to be taught a lesson, you know, Monkey.'

'No, I'm not going to give it back – until Amelia has sat on the bear's back and fished every single thing up out of his tummy,' said Monkey. 'It will take her hours! She'll hope she's fishing up her dress each time – but she'll never find that because I've got it! And when she's fished up simply *every*thing, I'll give her back the dress!'

Well, when she came back from the party, Amelia Jane saw the toys sitting on the floor round the fishing-

game with the rods, pretending to fish
for the cardboard fish that belonged
to the game – and, just as they had
guessed she would, she suddenly
thought that one of those little rods
would soon fish up her dress out of the
hole in the bear!

'Give me one!' she said, and
snatched a rod from Tom's hand. She

ran to the bear and climbed on his back. She let down the line through the hole.

'Don't! It tickles!' groaned the bear. But Amelia Jane took no notice. She suddenly jerked out the line, hoping to find her dress on the hook – but alas, it was the monkey's tail!

He snatched at it, grinning. 'Thanks! Just what I wanted!'

Amelia couldn't *think* why she didn't fish up her dress! Up came a shoe – and a piece of ribbon – and a tiny saucepan – and the sailor doll's hat. Goodness, how the toys stared! The marbles and coins didn't come, because the fishing rod didn't catch them – but all kinds of other things came up.

'My dress won't come!' said Amelia, beginning to cry. 'I've sat here for hours, and my arm aches, and I've fished up dozens of things – but not my dress!'

'Don't fish any more. It tickles me so,' said the bear.

'Oh, be quiet. That's about all you can say,' said Amelia.

Well, when she had sat fishing a bit longer even Monkey felt sorry for her – so he brought the dress out from the brick-box, where he had hidden it, and gave it to her.

'I fished it out before you got back

from the party,' he said. 'And we thought we'd make you fish out everything else before we told you, just to punish you!'

'Oh, my beautiful dress!' said Amelia Jane, very pleased. 'Oh, you *are* kind, Monkey. I'm very, very sorry I put everybody's things into the bear now. I never will again.'

'What about saying you're sorry to *me*?' grumbled the old bear. 'Tickling me like that – and I've *still* got something inside me, rattling away. Listen!' He ran a few centimetres on his wheels, and the toys could hear the marbles and coins inside him, rolling here and there. 'I don't like it,' said the bear. 'It's not right or proper. I want it stopped.'

'I'll stuff lots and lots of nice soft paper inside you,' said Amelia. 'That will stop them from rolling about. Half a minute!' Very soon she had pushed some sheets of tissue paper down the hole in his back. After that the marbles and coins didn't roll about any more, and the bear felt much more comfortable.

And now he knows something that nobody else knows! A little mouse found the hole in his back, and ran down into the soft paper inside. She made her nest there, and now there are five baby mice inside him.

He's so pleased! He isn't lonely any more. The mouse brings her babies out to see him whenever it's safe. They think the old bear is WONDERFUL, and he likes that.

'But don't you tickle me too much,' he says. 'Not *too* much! Else I might roll over with laughing and tip you all out! And, listen – if you want a good meal, you go and nibble the biscuit that Amelia Jane has hidden in the bead-box!'

Bother You, Amelia Jane!

'Amelia Jane – you're sitting in the very place where we want to have our race,' said the bear. 'Will you please move back a bit?'

'No,' said Amelia. 'I'm comfortable here.'

'We did say *please*,' said Tom the soldier.

'Well, I say *no, thank you*!' said
Amelia. 'NO, THANK YOU, I don't
want to move.'

'But Amelia, we're going to have a
race between the clockwork train, the
clockwork car and the clockwork fire-
engine,' said the sailor doll. 'And
where you're sitting is the only clear
space they can race in.'

'Well, I'm having a rest and I
shan't move,' said Amelia Jane, who
was feeling bad-tempered that day.
'Go away and don't bother me.'

'Amelia Jane, we're *going* to race
just here,' said Monkey. 'So at least
put your legs under you – you've got
them sticking out all over the place.'

'My legs always do,' said Amelia.
'And just keep your tail to yourself,
Monkey, and stop waggling it round
my feet.'

'She's hopeless,' said Teddy. 'Too
selfish for words! Well, let's have the
race anyhow, and tell the train and
the car and the fire-engine not to
bump into her feet – if they can help
it!'

The clockwork mouse giggled. 'If *I*
was in the race I'd run over both her
feet!' he said.

'One more word from you and I'll
take away your key, clockwork
mouse!' said Amelia Jane.

'You're rude,' said the sailor doll,

and began to wind up the fire-engine.
'Teddy, wind up the clockwork train –
and Monkey, wind up the car. We'll
start the race. If the fire-engine wins I
get a ride all round the playroom!'

'Right – and if *we* win with the
train or the car, *we* get free rides,'
said Teddy, and he and Monkey
began to wind up the train and the
car.

They set them in a straight row.
The clockwork mouse shouted 'One –
two – three – OFF!' and away went
the three clockwork toys.

'Once round the table – that's right
– the fire-engine's leading! Now twice
round!' cried Monkey. 'Look out,

Train, you nearly ran over Amelia Jane that time.'

'Train's leading – no, the car's catching it up!' shouted the sailor doll. 'Ooooh – look *out*, Fire-engine!'

The fire-engine was so excited that it swung round the table too sharply, ran too near Amelia Jane, caught the end of her toe with its bumper and turned right over on top of her. She squealed in fright.

'Oh! You did that on purpose! I know you did! Look at the hole you've made in my dress.'

'It didn't do it on purpose. It was just an accident!' shouted Sailor. 'You should have got out of the way as we told you!'

But Amelia Jane was in a temper and wouldn't listen. She kicked the fire-engine off her legs, and snatched at the key in its side. She took it right out, raised her arm – and flung the key away as far as she could. It went high up in the air, fell in a corner, slithered along a bit – and disappeared.

'Amelia! How dare you!' cried Monkey. 'You know keys mustn't be thrown about in case they're lost!

Quick, everyone, look for the key. The fire-engine can't go if we don't wind it up.'

Well, they looked and looked for the key, while Amelia Jane sulked and wouldn't help them at all.

'It serves you right!' she said. 'I'm *glad* the fire-engine's key is lost. I hope you never find it.'

Well, after that, the toys wouldn't speak to her, of course. 'It might have been *my* key she threw away,' said the clockwork mouse, trembling. 'Then I'd never be able to run about the nursery any more. Bad, wicked, naughty Amelia Jane!'

'If you talk like that, I'll *will* throw

your key away!' said Amelia, crossly, and the mouse didn't say another word.

Amelia Jane wasn't very happy the next day or two. Nobody talked to her, not even the rocking-horse, who usually talked to anyone, even himself. Nobody shared a sweet, nobody played a game with her. She began to feel very sorry for herself.

Then she saw the toys giggling together and wanted to share the joke.

But they quickly stuffed something under the bookcase when they saw her coming.

'What are you doing?' she said to the clockwork mouse who was poking his nose under the bookcase.

'Ooooh – I can see the lost fire-engine key!' he squeaked. 'Yes, I can! It's under here.'

'Well, get it then,' said Amelia Jane.

'We can't,' said the sailor doll. 'Nobody's arm is long enough to poke under and reach it.'

'And my tail isn't strong enough,' said Monkey. 'It's a pity you're such a bad-tempered person lately, Amelia Jane – not worth talking to, really! You

could have put your hand right under
the bookcase and got the key. Then
we'd have liked you much better.'

Well, Amelia Jane was feeling
tired of not being friends with anyone,
and she thought it might be a good
thing to get the lost key out. She bent
down to look underneath, and saw it,
away in the corner.

She put her arm under, and
reached it. She swished it out from
under the bookcase – and out
came something else as well!

Yes – a most
enormous spider! It
ran over Amelia's
arm, and then down her

back. She stood up at once and screamed. She was *so* afraid of spiders!

The toys laughed and laughed as they saw Amelia Jane running round the nursery chased by the big spider. 'You horrid things!' she cried. 'You knew the clockwork spider was there. That's why you made me put my arm underneath so that it would come after me! Tell it to go away, I don't like clockwork spiders.'

But the toys were laughing too much to listen. Amelia Jane stamped her foot at the spider.

'Go away. I'll take *your* key, too, and throw it out of the window. Go

away, I tell you. I don't like spiders.
I'll take your key!'

'Ho, ho, ho!' laughed Monkey.
'Take his key then, Amelia Jane, go
on, take it. We'd like to see you!'

'He hasn't *got* a key!' squeaked the
clockwork mouse. 'He's real! He's
alive, he isn't clockwork.'

Well, that was even worse! Amelia
Jane rushed into the toy-cupboard at
once, shut the door and squeezed
herself into the big brick-box, panting
and puffing loudly. The sailor doll
called to the spider.

'All right. You've scared her
enough. You can run up the wall and
out of the window – and thank you for

your help. Amelia Jane will be *much* better behaved now!'

She is, of course – but if she begins to be silly again the clockwork mouse will shout out, 'Here comes the spider, Amelia Jane!' And away she'll run into the toy-cupboard at once! Fancy being afraid of a *spider*!

It's Raining, Amelia Jane!

It was a great pity that Amelia Jane found the little teapot in the dolls' tea-set, because, of course, she at once wanted to fill it with something, so that she could pour out cups of tea or lemonade.

'She won't stop at pouring out cups of this and that,' said the teddy bear, gloomily. 'She'll be running after *us* with the teapot soon. I know Amelia Jane!'

The bear was right. Amelia Jane filled the teapot with water from the tap in the basin, and poured out full cups of tea for everyone. And then, of course, she wanted to be funny, and water people with the teapot!

'Oh do *stop* it, Amelia Jane!' said Tom the soldier, when Amelia poured the teapot water down his neck.

'It's raining!' said Amelia Jane, giggling. 'That's all! It's raining! Get your mackintosh, Tom.'

Then she watered the clockwork mouse as he lay asleep on the rug, and he was so scared that he jumped straight into the coal-scuttle and couldn't get out.

'Amelia Jane – it isn't funny! Stop this silly idea of yours!' said the clockwork clown. 'If you water *me* my clockwork may go rusty, and I shan't be able to walk or turn head-over-heels or anything!'

'Oh good!' said Amelia, and filled the teapot again at once. 'I'm tired of seeing you turn head-over-heels all the time! Here I come!'

And she ran at the poor clockwork clown, who had to get inside the empty brick-box and hold the lid tightly over him till the monkey came

131

to tell him that Amelia Jane had watered the baby doll instead.

'Just wait till *we* get hold of that teapot!' said the clown. But Amelia Jane gave him no chance of that. She put the teapot safely beside her even when she went to sleep!

And then the teddy bear made an exciting discovery. There was a little cupboard in the playroom that was usually kept tightly shut, because in it were all kinds of things put away by the children's mother – things she wanted to keep for the children, or to store out of their way.

One morning she went to the cupboard to get a paint-box she had left there for a birthday present. She shut the little cupboard door – but it slid open again, and she didn't notice.

So, when she had gone out of the room and everything was quiet again, the bear went to peep inside the cupboard. It was a most exciting place.

There was a little work-box there with a thimble, needles, pins, scissors and

all kinds of things. There was a pile of new books, stored there in case one of the children was ill and wanted new stories to read. There were two or three games to play – and then, right at the back, the bear saw something that made him prick up his little blunt ears.

'A watering-can! A small watering-can! The one that's used at Christmas time to water the bowls of bulbs in the playroom. Aha! Now I wonder if I can think of an idea to punish Amelia Jane!'

The bear got right inside the cupboard and thought hard.

He peeped out after a time, and

saw that Amelia Jane had climbed into the baby doll's cot for a sleep. It was a terrible squash for the baby doll when she did that, but Amelia Jane never bothered about things like that!

The teddy bear beckoned to the monkey, and he came scampering up, his long tail behind him. The bear showed him the watering-can and whispered into his ear. The monkey nodded and chuckled.

'Yes! Good idea! I'll do it! It'll serve Amelia Jane right!'

'You see, you are the only toy that can climb about everywhere, and leap and spring from place to place,' said the bear. 'And you are strong too –

you can easily carry this little watering-can with you. All you have to do is to wait till Amelia Jane waters someone with the teapot, and says "It's raining, it's raining!" and then *you* tip up the watering-can, and water *her* – and we'll ALL shout out "Yes, it's raining, it's raining!"'

'And all the time it will really be me, sitting up on the table or on the side-board or chest, tipping up the can!' said Monkey with a grin. 'You do get good ideas, Bear. I shall *love* to do that! I won't let Amelia Jane see me.'

'We shall all have a lot of good laughs,' said the bear. 'Here's the can. Go and fill it while Amelia is asleep in the baby doll's cot. Then hop up on the table-top and wait!'

Monkey filled the little can. Then up he leapt to the table-top and sat there, waiting. All the toys were excited, and simply *longed* for Amelia Jane to wake up.

She awoke at last, feeling mischievous as she always did after a nice long sleep. She jumped down from the cot with the teapot, which, as usual, had been beside her. She stood on the chair beside the basin and filled the teapot full. Aha – now look out, you toys – here comes the rain!

The toys stood and watched her. The bear had put on a little

mackintosh, and had said that he
would run away from Amelia, and go
round the table, so that Monkey could
do a little watering from above. So, as
soon as Amelia jumped down from
the chair, he began to run – and of
course she ran after him with the
teapot!

'It's raining, it's raining!' she cried,
and poured the water over his back.
And, at that very moment, Monkey
peeped over the table-top and tilted
his little watering-can! Splishy-splash!
Splishy-splash! My goodness me,
what a shock for Amelia Jane!

'It's raining, it's raining!' yelled all
the toys in delight! Amelia Jane

spluttered and gasped.
She was dripping from
head to foot. She ran
across the room to
shelter under the
sideboard, but, with one
leap, Monkey sprang
from the table to the
sideboard, and before
Amelia could get
underneath he had
watered her again!

'It's raining! It's
pouring!' yelled the
toys, and Tom the
soldier laughed so much
that he had to lie down

and roll on the floor.

Well, Amelia was most astonished, especially as she seemed to be the only wet toy, except for the bear she had watered with the teapot. She had to take off her wet clothes and put them in a patch of sunshine to dry. She put on her little blue dressing-gown, and felt very cross.

The toys went on giggling for a long time. 'What a downpour that was!' said the bear.

'Dear me, quite a rain-storm,' said the clown. 'I was surprised it didn't thunder too.'

'Well, Amelia told the bear it was raining, and it certainly was,' said the baby doll. 'What a joke!'

Amelia Jane lost her temper. 'It's not a joke!' she said, getting up. 'It was very bad luck to get soaked like that. I'll just water you all again, then you'll stop laughing at me!'

She went to fill her teapot and Monkey got ready on the table-top again. His can was still half full! He gave a sudden giggle. Oh dear – this really was very funny.

The bear gave the clockwork mouse a push, and he ran in front of Amelia. 'Don't water me, don't water me!' he cried.

'It's raining, it's raining!' shouted Amelia Jane as usual, and ran after

141

him towards the table.

Splishy-splashy-splishy-splashy –
Monkey emptied half the water over
the side of the table on to Amelia
Jane. She gasped and
spluttered and
dropped the
teapot. It broke
into pieces – oh
dear!

'It's raining,
it's pouring, it's
simply pelting
down!' shouted
the toys, dancing about in delight, as
they saw poor dripping Amelia Jane.
She ran to the toy-cupboard but

Monkey leapt to the top of it and emptied the rest of the can of water on to the big doll. Goodness, what a waterfall!

Amelia crouched down in a corner of the cupboard. Her hair was very wet and little trickles of water ran down her neck. She sneezed.

'What a rain-storm!' said Tom, peeping into the cupboard. 'Why do you keep on going out in the pouring rain, Amelia?'

'I don't,' said Amelia. 'How do *I* know when it's going to pour with rain?'

'Well, you always call out that it's raining just before the rain pours down on you,' said the bear, with a giggle. 'I think you must *make* it rain, Amelia. It serves you right. You've poured teapot rain on *us* every day, so you shouldn't mind if you get rained on too! Ha, ha, ha!'

'You've broken the teapot,' said the clown. 'That's very careless of you. It will have to be stuck together with glue.'

'Well, stick it, then,' said Amelia, with another sneeze. 'I shan't use it any more. I'm tired of it. And what's more, I'm going to go round dressed in my rubber boots, and my mackintosh, *and* hold up my umbrella till these sudden storms have stopped!'

And will you believe it, she goes parading round the playroom dressed just like that every day – and old Monkey sometimes gives her a beautiful rain-storm so as not to disappoint her. You should hear the toys shouting then.

'Look out, Amelia Jane! Here comes the rain! Mind the puddles on the carpet. It's raining again!'

Amelia Jane and the Keys

Now, one day Amelia Jane discovered something very peculiar, something that nobody had discovered before. It came about like this.

The clockwork robot had lost his key. He didn't even know he had lost it till his clockwork ran down and he couldn't walk – and when he asked

Amelia Jane to wind him up, she couldn't because his key was not in his back.

'You've lost your key, Robot,' said Amelia Jane. 'Where did you drop it?'

'Oh dear – I really don't know,' said Robot, upset. 'It might be anywhere!'

So Amelia Jane and the toys looked all over the floor, and they looked in

the toy-cupboard, too – but there was no key to be found.

'You'll just have to sit still all the time and watch us playing,' said the clockwork mouse sadly. 'You should have been more careful with your key!'

'Lend him yours,' said Amelia Jane to the mouse.

'No, certainly not,' said the mouse. 'It might get lost, too. And, anyway, it wouldn't fit.'

'Motor-car man – lend Robot *your* key!' said Amelia Jane. But the little tin man in the clockwork motor-car wouldn't.

'No,' he said. 'My car key might

break if you tried to wind up Robot with it, you know it might. Don't you dare to touch it. If you do, I'll run my car over your toes!'

'All right, all right,' said Amelia Jane. She looked round for some more clockwork toys, but by now they had all gone to hide, afraid that Amelia Jane might give Robot their keys.

The big doll was cross. She liked Robot because he was always ready to play games with her – but if he couldn't be wound up he would have to sit still all the time. Amelia went to the toy-cupboard, and looked inside to see if any other clockwork toy was there.

There was just one – and that was the little jumping rabbit, fast asleep. Whenever he was wound up he jumped here and there all over the floor, and the toys loved him very much.

Amelia Jane didn't wake him. She slid her hand behind his back and took out his key, very, very gently. She went over to Robot with it.

'I've got a key,' she said. 'It's the jumping rabbit's. I'm sure it will fit you. Keep still and I'll wind you up.'

She had to force the key a little, but at last it went into the hole in Robot's back. She began to wind him up.

'The key feels different!' he said in alarm. 'It's not winding me up properly, Amelia Jane. It makes me feel peculiar. Stop winding me.'

'Don't be silly,' said Amelia Jane, and went on winding till she could wind no more. 'There – now you can run about again, Robot. Let's have a game.'

Robot stood up to run – but what

was this? He wasn't running – he was jumping like a rabbit. Hoppity-hop, hoppity-hop! All the toys stared at him in surprise.

'Look at Robot – he's hopping like the rabbit!' cried the clockwork mouse, running up. 'Why are you doing that, Robot? Oh, you really do look funny!'

'I *can't* walk – I have to hop!' groaned Robot. 'What's come over me? Oooh – *that* was a big hop! I nearly landed in the fireplace!'

Amelia Jane began to laugh. She guessed at once what had happened! The rabbit's key was different from Robot's – that must be it. It always made the rabbit hop – and now it was making Robot hop! Amelia Jane laughed and laughed.

And then a wonderful idea slid into her mischievous mind. Ooooh! Suppose she managed to get the

clockwork clown's key – when he was
wound up with *his* key he turned
head-over-heels! And OOOOOOH!
Suppose she put it into the clockwork
motor-car's keyhole, and wound up
the little car – would the car turn
head-over-heels?

Amelia Jane chuckled. She just
couldn't wait to try out her ideas!
She would have to watch her chance
and take the keys when people
weren't looking.

Well, by the end of the next day
Amelia Jane had
somehow managed to
collect six keys!
She managed this

rather cleverly. She went up to the clockwork train and offered to wind it up – and put the key into her pocket when she had finished. She kindly wound up the clockwork mouse – and pocketed his key, too. Then she wound up the toy motor-car for the little toy driver, and that key went into her pocket as well.

She had the rabbit's key, too, and the clockwork clown's – and dear me, she found Robot's key as well, under one of the mats. Aha! Now she would have some fun!

The little driver in the clockwork motor-car wanted winding up before anyone else did – his clockwork had

run down because he had taken so
many toys for a ride round the
nursery floor.

'Hey! My key's gone!' he shouted
suddenly. 'What's happened to it?
Amelia Jane, did you put it into your
pocket by mistake?'

'Dear me – here it is!' said Amelia,
rattling the keys in her pocket. She
pulled out one – it was the key
belonging to the clockwork clown, who
turned head-over-heels as he went
along. What would happen when she
used it for the toy motor-car?

She ran to the car and put the key
into the hole. It was rather small, but
Amelia pushed it right in and began to

wind. R-r-r-r-r-r-r! R-r-r-r-r-r-r!
R-r-r-r-r-r!

'There – you're wound up!' she
said to the little driver. 'Off you go!'

And off went the car – but what
was happening? It was turning head-
over-heels as it went! Bumpity-bump,
bumpity-bump!

The toys stared in astonishment.
What was the car doing? The driver
yelled in fright, 'What's happening?
We're turning head-over-heels!'

Amelia Jane laughed and laughed!
She had to go into a corner and stuff
her hanky into her mouth because she
laughed so much. She didn't want the
toys to guess yet that she had mixed

up the keys. No – she would wind up a few more things first!

The car went on turning head-over-heels till the clockwork ran down. The little driver was angry and upset. His tin hat had been bent as the car turned over and over, and he felt very giddy. He sat in the car, which was now quite still, hardly daring to touch the steering-wheel in case he was thrown head-over-heels again.

Amelia Jane waited eagerly for the train-driver to call her next. At last she heard him. 'Amelia! Have you seen my key? You were the last to wind me up, and I'm sure you must have taken it by mistake.'

'I'll look,' said Amelia Jane, trying not to laugh. 'Ah – here it is!' She took a key from her pocket and put it into the keyhole of the clockwork train. R-r-r-r-r-r-r! R-r-r-r-r-r-r! She wound it up as fast as she could. There – the key would not turn any more.

'Right,' said Amelia Jane, and picked up the guard's green flag and waved it. 'All clear! Off you go, train-driver!'

The train began to run over the nursery floor – and then it acted in a most peculiar manner! You see, Amelia had wound it up with the key belonging to the jumping rabbit – and now it was jumping up and down as it went. Jumpity-jump, hoppity-hop, jumpity-jump!

'Hey – what are you doing, train?' shouted the surprised train-driver. 'Stop this jumping! You'll upset your carriages!'

But the train couldn't stop jumping, of course. It leapt here and there, shaking and hopping and clanking – and all the toys stared in wonder. What could be happening in the nursery today?

One of the carriages jumped so high that it fell over, and that brought the train to a standstill, though it still trembled and shook as if it wanted to jump in the air again. The train-driver mopped his forehead.

'I don't understand it,' he said. 'It's most peculiar – very frightening. What are you laughing at, Amelia Jane? This isn't funny.'

'Oh, it is, it is!' laughed Amelia, holding her sides. 'You don't know how funny it is! Oh my, oh my, I've never laughed so much in my life!'

Then will you believe it, she wound up the little clockwork mouse with the train key – and instead of running along the floor at his own gentle speed, he found himself racing along as fast as a train! He bumped into this and bumped into that, and soon his

nose was so bruised that he
began to cry!

'What's happening! I
must be going along at
sixty miles an hour! I don't
like it, I don't like it!' he
cried, and bumped straight
into Jumbo the elephant,
almost knocking him over.

'Steady there, steady,'
said Jumbo, surprised, and
caught the little mouse by the
tail to hold him still. 'What's the
hurry?'

'There isn't any hurry, but I
can't stop myself going at top

speed!' wailed the mouse. 'Hold me safe, Jumbo, hold me safe!'

'Ho-ho-ho-ho!' roared Amelia Jane, and tears of laughter ran down her cheeks. 'Oh, this is the funniest thing I've ever seen. Jumbo, it's a pity you haven't got a keyhole – I'd wind you up and make you turn head-over-heels – how funny you would look!'

Jumbo marched up to Amelia Jane and put his long trunk down into her pocket. He drew it out full of keys and jangled them high in the air.

'So *that's* what you've been doing!' he trumpeted angrily. 'You've used the wrong keys for all the clockwork toys.

My word, if *you* had a hole for a key, Amelia, I'd wind you up with every single one of these keys – and watch you run and jump and turn head-over-heels all at the same time. Here, toys – come and get your right keys – and don't you ever let Amelia Jane wind you up in future, or she'll play the very same trick again!'

Nobody would talk to Amelia Jane after that. They turned their backs on her. The dolls'-house dolls didn't ask her to share their sweets. The other toys frowned when she came near. Nobody would play with her or even answer when she spoke to them.

'Please!' she said at last. 'I'm

sorry. I won't do it again. I really am very *very* sorry. Do be nice to me again, please do.'

Well, at last they all forgave her, and for at least a week Amelia Jane was good and polite and quiet – but every now and again she went into the toy-cupboard and shut the door. And when she was inside she began to laugh. How she laughed. 'Ho-ho-ho-ho-ho-ho! Ho-ho-ho-ho-ho-ho!'

'*Whatever* can she be laughing at now?' wondered the toys anxiously. 'Is she up to any more mischief?'

No – she wasn't. She was just remembering something funny – but she wouldn't tell the toys what it was.

I know what she was laughing at, though – don't you?

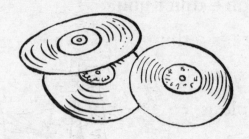

Amelia Jane and the Records

'Do come out of the toy-cupboard,
Amelia Jane,' said the sailor doll.
'Whatever are you doing? You keep
throwing out all kinds of things and
making an awful mess out here.'

'I'm looking for something,' said
Amelia Jane.

'What is it?' asked Tom the soldier.

'I don't know what it's called – but it's a thing that sings and plays music,' said Amelia.

'Oh – you mean the toy record-player,' said the teddy bear. 'I haven't seen that for ages. The children never use it now.'

'They used to,' said the clockwork mouse. 'They used to play it every day, and when they played "Three Blind Mice", I was frightened and ran into the toy-cupboard.'

'Baby!' said Amelia Jane.

'He's not,' said the pink cat. '*I* couldn't bear one of the songs, either. When the record played "Ding Dong Bell, Pussy's in the Well", *I* was frightened. I don't like to hear about cats swimming in deep wells.'

'And I hated the one about someone called Mother Hubbard,' said the white dog. 'She had a dog, and he must have been so hungry, poor thing, because there was never anything in her cupboard for him. Never. It was always bare. It used to make *me* feel hungry when I heard the song.'

'Oooh – I wish I could find the record-player,' said Amelia Jane gleefully. 'I'd play *all* those songs. I'd like to see the clockwork mouse, the pink cat and the white dog all shiver and shake together!'

'You're unkind,' said the sailor doll. 'I'm glad there wasn't a song about *me*. You'd play that, too, I suppose!'

Amelia Jane rummaged about in the cupboard for all she was worth. She must, she really must find that old, toy record-player! It would be such fun to play it and annoy the toys.

She found it at last, carefully packed in its little square cardboard box. Amelia Jane gave a squeal of delight.

'I've got it! Here it is, look!' she

said. She took it carefully from its box, and carried it out of the cupboard on to the carpet. She set it down, and all the toys came round to look at it.

'That's it,' said Tom the soldier.

'Don't play it, please don't,' said the clockwork mouse. 'It might play that horrid "Blind Mice" song – or the "Dickory Dock" one. I didn't like that either, because the mouse in it was afraid when the clock struck one so loudly.'

'I'm certainly going to play it,' said Amelia, and she switched on the record-player. But nothing happened, except that a small, round disc in the middle went round and round and round, making a little creaking noise.

'It doesn't sing or play,' said Amelia Jane in disgust. 'It must be broken.'

'It isn't,' said the teddy bear, who had a very good memory. 'I remember what the children used to do when they wanted the record-player to play a tune. They took a funny little round thing, black it was, with round ring-markings – and they set it there, on that thing that is turning round.'

'Oh yes – and they turned it on to play,' said Tom, remembering too. 'And the needle went round and round and made the tune come. Like magic, it was.'

'Oh – so *that's* how a record-player works,' said Amelia Jane, delighted. 'I'd quite forgotten.'

Then the teddy bear pointed to a little drawer set at the bottom of the record-player. 'The records are in there,' he said. 'The little black discs with lines on. I don't know how music gets into them, but it's there. The needle brings it out.'

'Oh, don't play it, don't play it,' begged the clockwork mouse, and the pink cat said the same thing. Amelia Jane took no notice at all, of course. She opened the little drawer – and there were the old records just as the bear had said. She took one and slipped it in place, and then put it on to play – and at once music filled the air.

'Wonderful!' said the bear. 'It's the "Teddy Bear's Picnic" tune. Dum-dum-dumpty-dumpty, dum-dum-dum – dance with me, sailor doll!'

Amelia Jane tried all the little records one by one; when she came to the 'Three Blind Mice' record she played it gleefully, watching the little clockwork mouse.

'I don't like it, I don't like it!' he

squeaked, and when Amelia Jane picked up a pencil and pretended to cut his tail off, he was really frightened. 'She cut off his tail with a carving-knife!' sang naughty Amelia Jane, and sawed at the poor clockwork mouse's tail with the pencil.

She was just as bad with the pink cat, and played 'Ding Dong Bell, Pussy's in the Well' at least twenty times, till everyone was very very tired of it, especially the pink cat.

'I feel as if I'm wet through,' he said. 'All that singing about falling into the well! Oh dear – now she's playing the "Mother Hubbard" tune, and the poor toy dog is looking quite hungry! Really, can't someone stop Amelia Jane!'

But nobody could. She played that little record-player all the time, and everyone got very very bored with it. The sailor doll found some cotton-wool and stuffed up his ears, and soon everyone was trying to do the same.

In the end the sailor doll slid out of the window and down the tree outside to call on the tiny goblin who lived in

a hole at the bottom of the tree.

'Hallo,' said the goblin in surprise. 'I don't often have a visit from *you*. Is there something you want?'

'Yes,' said the sailor doll and told him about Amelia Jane and the record-player. 'You see, she keeps on and on playing things we don't like. So now we want something *we* can play that she'll hate. Can you think of an idea?'

'Easy,' said the goblin. 'But I want payment, please.'

'Oh dear, we haven't any money,' said the sailor doll.

'No money,' said the goblin. 'Marbles! I love marbles! But last week my cousin Sneaky took my marbles and rolled every one of them down a wormhole – and the worm won't give them back. Can you give me marbles in payment for my help?'

'I think so,' said the sailor. 'But you'll have to help us first. We don't give goblins payment till they've done what they promised, you know. You're rather tricky little things! How are you going to help?'

'I'll make a few records myself,' said the goblin with a grin. 'I know enough magic to do that. Then you play them on the record-player, and see what Amelia Jane says when she hears them! I can tell you that she won't like them!'

'Good,' said the sailor doll. 'Come up the tree to our window tomorrow night, when the moon is full. Give me the records, and I'll hand you the marbles. Goodbye for now!'

Well, the next night the sailor doll was sitting waiting on the window-sill when a little hand came in at the bottom of the window, holding a few records, just like the ones on the toy record-player. The sailor doll took them quietly, and put four good marbles into the goblin's bony hand. Amelia Jane didn't notice anything.

The sailor doll was excited. He waited till Amelia Jane had turned away for a moment from the record-player, and then slid the goblin's records on to the pile of records. He winked at the other toys.

Amelia Jane took the top record and put it on. 'This should be "Ding Dong Bell" again,' she said. 'If you feel *too* wet, Pink Cat, I'll lend you my hanky to dry yourself!'

The disc began to turn round and round. Music came out – and then the voice of the goblin sounded, loud and clear, singing rather a rude song.

'Amelia Jane is very plain,
Her nose is far too big,
And when she speaks
She grunts and squeaks

Just like a little pig!

Oh, haha-haha – ha-ha-HA,

Just like a little pig!'

'Well! What record is *that*?' cried Amelia Jane angrily. 'How rude! I'll take it off at once!'

But the toys wouldn't let her. 'Play it again,' begged the clockwork mouse. 'I want to join in the "ha-ha-HA!" bit.'

So they played it again and shouted 'Oh, haha-haha – ha-ha-HA, just like a little pig!' at the tops of their voices.

Amelia Jane was almost in tears. She snatched the record off at last and put on another one. But that was just as bad! The toys listened to the goblin's mischievous song in delight.

'*Amelia Jane is very vain,*
She struts about all day,
Her tongue she wags
And boasts and brags,
We wish she'd go away!
Oh, haha-haha – ha-ha-HA,
We wish she'd go away!'

Amelia Jane couldn't believe her ears! The toys joined

in the chorus, of course, and Amelia grew very red in the face. She took off that record very quickly, and, with a sulky look, put another on at once. I can't understand this, she thought. I've not heard *these* before!

The third record whisked merrily round and round, and the goblin's voice rose again – what a wicked little voice it was!

> *'Amelia Jane is bad again,*
> *She really is a bore,*
> *There'll come a day*
> *When we shall say*
> *Goodbye for evermore!*
> *Oh, haha-haha – ha-ha-HA,*
> *Goodbye for evermore!*

Oh, haha-haha – ha-ha-HA,
Goodbye for evermore!'

The toys joined in and kept on and on with the haha lines, waving to Amelia Jane as if they were saying goodbye. She suddenly burst into tears and stopped the record-player.

'Don't! I don't like it!' she said. 'What horrid songs! How did they get there?'

'They're no worse than the ones you've been playing that *we* didn't like!' said the clockwork mouse. 'Oh, haha-haha – ha-ha-HA, goodbye for evermore, Amelia Jane!'

'DON'T!' said Amelia! 'Don't say goodbye to me. I want to stay here. I'm *going* to stay here. And I want you to be friends with me, please, please, PLEASE! I'm sorry I kept on playing things you didn't like. Oh dear – *is* my nose far too big? And *do* I boast and brag – and *am* I a bore?'

'We'll tell you the answers in a day or two,' said Tom with a grin. He took the three records made by the goblin and gave them to the sailor doll. 'Hide them, in case we need to play them again,' he said.

'You won't need to,' said Amelia Jane in a small voice. 'See – I'm going to pack the record-player into its box and put it away. Don't let's ever play the records again!'

'We'll see,' said the sailor doll solemnly. 'We'll see about that in a day or two, Amelia Jane.'

'Let's play a nice game together,' said Amelia, longing to be friends. 'Where are the marbles? Let's play marbles and roll them all over the floor!'

But there were no marbles to be found – and nobody liked to tell Amelia Jane that the goblin had them and was having a wonderful time rolling them up and down the wormholes in the garden!

She's big! She's bad!

She's the terror of the toy cupboard... and she's back!

More adventures from Amelia Jane.

 EGMONT